Copyright © July 2023 b
Cover design by Sylver (

The scanning, uploading
permission is theft of the author's intellectual property.

If you would like permission to use ideas from the Introduction of this book (other than review purposes), please contact silverdacutie@aol.com.

Thank you for your support of author's rights.

A Teacher's Perspective

As states in the US continue to ban TikTok, the social media app grows in popularity globally. Let this book become a part of the conversation over TikTok being a threat as the greatest fear of the app only lives in those are who the most unfamiliar with it.

My cousin and I (both Millennials) love TikTok but for different reasons. She uses the app to stay up to date on fashion, movies and food. I use the app to help motive myself, learn about plants and gather information not offered on regular news. Kids today have different reasons for using the app too. Have you ever stopped to ask them why?

Whether you like the use of it or not, the app's purpose has evolved. It now offers more than just an opportunity to waste time, or a tunnel for the Chinses to spy on us. TikTok has become a multimillion-dollar business were "the little man" voices their opinions or learns from others who do. It's no longer for just kids, but *anyone* who wants to advertise, influence or reach a larger audience. TikTok has changed how commercials are produced and distributed as influencers are more relatable than today celebrities. Yes, there's the occasionally monologue or an off-beat renegade, but if you use the app regularly you'll notice that it's creating trends throughout the real world with a landscape built by all. No wonder, they want to kill the app. The elite are no longer in charge.

In my search for videos to include in this book, I found even more than I thought I knew. Using a dummy account, I noticed users are now posting videos that spread social-awareness over bigger issues like human trafficking and signs to avoid being trafficked, opposing opinions over current political ideas that can help foster independent thought, and use of spiritual manifestation over acting out and revenge. These are all important ideas that promote self-regulation and independence, which I myself never learned until I was in college. And if it weren't for TikTok, I would have never known how socially aware our kids are as a classroom teacher. That's something that Facebook, Twitter, and Instagram have yet to do.

If you are worried about your privacy or being spied on, chances are you should delete your Facebook or Twitter instead, as both companies have been sued for selling your information for a profit. If China followed suit, tracking my Amazon purchases, then honestly, so what?

The only reason people are mad at TikTok is because they aren't directly benefitting from the use of the app. To them, their competitors are, and yes, kids can be considered competitors in this case (how many followers do they have). Adults have no problem with Chinese products, Chinese intelligence, Chinese aid to help save our economy, but for some reason, this Chinese *app* is getting a lot of attention. The kids would could that "sus."

Don't be distracted by the issues being forced onto your screens. Get engaged. Check the app out for yourself if you haven't already. Check everything. And if not, hopefully this book can help you understand there is always an opposing opinion, and that's what makes America great.

Teach kids discernment, not fear. Let's get back to teaching digital citizenship in the classroom. That way, when the next app comes around (which it will), no matter who creates it, we as adults can trust in our kids and spend our time debating more important issues that better protect them. School safety and teacher support would be two great places to start.

The rest of the book includes TikToks that backup the claim that TikTok has many purposes and allows the average-joe an opportunity to be heard globally without US government benefit.

All I did was format them for this book, as I see them in my mind.

Enjoy!

Karma

spoken words by *Black Willy Wonka,*
personality, filmmaker, vibe

<u>Instrumental</u>: *I Got 5 On It* - Tethered Mix from US

When a bird is alive, it eats ants.
When the bird is dead, ants eats the bird.
Time and circumstance can change at any time,
That's why you don't devalue or hurt anyone in life.
Because, you maybe powerful today,
But remember, *time* is more powerful than *you*.

One tree makes a million matchsticks,
But only one matchstick is needed to burn a million trees.
That's why you gotta be good and do good.
That's Karma.

One Thing

spoken words by *lei.lyn*

Jesus is telling you to stop trying to do everything and do the one thing.

So, there's this story in the bible about two sisters. The older is Martha, and the younger is Mary. Jesus comes to visit both sisters and Martha is in the kitchen slaving away. She's making sure all of the food is prepared, she's trying to get drinks ready. Like you could imagine her trying to make sure everything is good for Jesus. She's testing the food, making sure it tastes good. All of the things. All while Mary is sitting at Jesus's feet, just listening to him talk. So as Martha is running in and out of the kitchen, she finally stops and she's like "Jesus, do you not see me doing all this, like can you tell her to help me? And she's frustrating cause she's over there sitting at your feet while I'm running in and out of the kitchen. Can you have her help? God responds was "Martha, you are worried and troubled about many things, but one thing is needed and Mary has chosen that good part which will not be taking away from her." So, while Martha is focused on serving, Mary is focused on receiving. And Jesus is saying I came here not to be feed. I appreciate your efforts. But I came to feed. Don't you know that I'm the multiplied fish and loaves to feed a multitude?"

Sometimes the hardest thing for us to do is just to stop. Stop your own efforts and just rely on God's unmerited favor. Once you learn to do the one thing, once you learn to listen to God and to really sit at his feet, you won't have to worry about everything else going on. So like Mary, focus on Jesus and just sit at Gods feet. Don't be troubled or overwhelmed with everything that going and everything you have to do and everything you have to get done. God delights in serving you through his unmerited favor. So, it's time to for you to stop working and to just sit at God's feet and receive him.

Rejection

video posted by *Aarondeheediah1*

───────────

Watch this:

"People every day rejects things they cannot afford."

When they rejected you, it didn't mean that you were valueless. It meant that they recognized that they could not afford you.

So, they left you, and you misinterpret their exit as an admission that you were worthless. But it actually was actually an admission on their part, that you were *priceless*.

You Are Not the One to Drop

spoken words by *Brooke Keith,*
of *Brooke Keith Ministries*

You need to just stop don't scroll, don't go to the dog video. I need you to hear me. No matter if you believe, no matter if you believe like me or even if you like me, I got something important to tell you: You are not the one to drop.

Because here's what's gonna happen. When they drop you, you do not break. You're like a phoenix and you always rise from the ashes and breaking is not the scary part. The scary part to you is doing it over and over and over again and when will I find capable hands? well honey, capable hands are only from above. So i need you to remember something for me. Promise me. If you never see me again, if you never pass this way again, you will remember the crazy lady on the internet that wasn't all that crazy, and told you that you cannot be dropped in the way they think that you can.

Whether it be a friend or family or relationship or a business, when they drop you, you will not break, but they will. When favor leaves a lie, favor leaves fast. And I don't know if you never known anybody who didn't know God for themselves but they love the God in you. And they wouldn't admit it and they might not know it, but it's just like when your around, good things happen. When you're around, all the bad stuff is just better. When you're around, all the roadblocks became roadways. You became the bridge. So, when they drop you, they drop the favor, and it breaks their heart. It shatters their shell. It shatters their masks and all that they're left with is the misery again.

I never want you to fear being dropped, baby, because you were made well. You heard of that company Made Well? You are made well. You are stitched well. The father knew that people would mishandle you not because you are made to be mishandled. Not because you're not of high importance, because baby, you are. You are couture. You are made by the father. You are hand crafted. Not because you're not important but because when you are anointed honey, they will carry you like the football and so they can't carry you no more because the anointing is so heavy. And one day, they might say something like "you're just too difficult" or "you're just too much." Then they can go find less.

Let them drop you. Cause I promise you're gonna rise back up. I promise they're gonna look at you one day from wherever you are that God has placed you, and they're gonna be like "man, I shouldn't have dropped that." And you're not gonna be broken. You're gonna be shining like all the beautiful glass that you are. Transparent for the world to see your story so other women know that when we are dropped, we do not break. W only rise further to shatter more glass ceilings 'cause that's who God called you to be.

Seek to Understand

spoken words by *Albaner C. Eugene*

_____

My father was somebody who would say things that hurt me but he wasn't trying to be hurtful. And until I understood him that's when I got relief for myself.

You say, your parents says "what's that gone do for you? That job ain't gonna get you no money." You trying to be understood here is *wow. my close people don't support me. My close people who not for me* because you just want validation. You just want affirmation.

But if you seek to understand them you hear "okay, this is my mom or my dad. They just want me to have a certain level of stability and there's a little anxious that either I'm not searching for stability or I don't have the proper tools to get stability. They do support my dreams they just don't want me while I'm pursing my dreams to not find stability because if they die, what will happen to their little girl, to their son?"

Until you understand that, you will always feel like they just *they just don't get me*. So, the relief doesn't come from you being understood, the relief comes from *oh, I understand them.* It's not personal.

And I know it's hard when you live with people. That's the, that, living with people talk is definitely difficult. You got everybody at homes gotta learn how to communicate with each other.

Indifferent

a TikTok Scene,

spoken words by *Unknown*

Scene: Two guys are in the mall. One guy is black, he is recording the other. The other is white, with glasses. He has a modest face.

Black Guy: People are just walking in front like we aren't even recording.

White Guy: Yeahhh, it happens. People are people. None of its intentional. Never attribute to malice what you can attributed to incompetence. It's far more likely that their all in their own worlds, doing their own thing. They're not paying attention to the world around them and we all do it every day whether you're driving, or walking down the street. All of our lives are just as complex as everybody else's. Everything you have going on, they have going on. Nobody know what everyone else is going through. We also need to be a little more self-aware and aware of the world around us.

Black Guy: (nods in agreement for several seconds in silence) That was deep.

White Guy: (shrugs) you gotta look deep to find the deep things. If all you ever do in your life is stay at the surface, you'll never find anything worth exploring.

Black Guy: (silence for a few seconds) Are you real?

White Guy: I try to be.

Black Guy: Are you a AI?

White Guy: (politely) No, not at all.

End Scene.

The Universe Is on Your Side

spoken words by *Esther Hicks,*
The Teachings of Abraham Hicks

———————

It's all coming together for me,

because my life is supposed to go well, and things are

supposed to be good for me,

and life is supposed to be fun.

And I'm supposed to feel at ease,

and things are supposed to work out for me.

And things are working out for me

and when I look at it, more is working out than isn't.

DO NOT TOUCH IT

video posted by *AwarenessRITENow*,
video stars *Egypt Sherrod from HGTV*

───────────────

Okay babies, it's late, I'm out getting a tank of gas, and I um watched a man put this on the gas handle and I just had to run over and tell the little girl not to touch it. Um, but I watched him do this (shows he gas pump with a tissue placed in the gap were a hand would normally go). do you see the tissue? You see it? So, um, if you ever find yourself at a gas station and a tissue is on the handle, or you come back to your car and you see a tissue under the handle or your vehicle, DO NOT TOUCH IT. At All. Because, this is what traffickers are doing. Their putting a toxin on the tissue and then their putting it in a place where you have to touch and their waiting for you to pass out. Okay, and so this little girl pulled up getting ready to fill up her tank, and the guy is literally sitting in the car right there (looks over to here right).

(She tries to show him by turning her back to him on portrait mode) He just walked away because he heard me talking about it, but pay attention. Stay alert.

(A man in a blue hat in the background walks by in the background)

Keep Going

spoken words by *Zoe Austrie,*
Mindset Guide

Speak light into your life, keep going.

Speak as though it already is because it's happening, keep going.

Don't stop, don't get discouraged, keep going.

Stay in your lane, keep going.

You got this, I promise, keep going.

Everything that is meant for you is already yours, keep going.

Keep going.

Comparison for what,

compare yourself to who?

Not even who you've been.

You are brand-new,

you are completely renewed.

Get to know this version of yourself,

stand in it ten toes down.

Keep going.

Keep *growing*.

You got this!

Eat the Rich

spoken words by *The History Wizard*

> Replying to fhdjdhdhd2's comment: Could you prove that all two thousand of the billionaires are evil people.

This comment is asking if I could prove that all 2,000 of the billionaires are evil people. Yeah, yeah I can. It's not even very hard.

So, first let's put a billion into perspective. One million seconds is about 12 days. One billion seconds is just under 32 years. Which means that if you earned $1 every single second and never spent any of it, it would take you about 32 years to earn a single billion dollars. If you earned 5,000 dollars a day from the time that Columbus started his infamous voyage, it would take you about 527 years to earn a single billion dollars. And there are people out there with *multiple* billions of dollars.

Based on that math, we can conclude that there's no ethical way to acquire a billion dollars because there's no physically possible way to earn that money solely through the value of your own labor. Which means that in order to become a billionaire you have to steal the labor value of thousands, if not millions of people. And we know that this is the case because between 1979 and 2021 the average productivity, meaning the average amount of labor value produce by the workers has increased by 64.6% (shows screenshot of data mentioned). Meanwhile, the average wage of workers has only increased by about 17.3%. That's a difference of nearly 50% labor value. So, already billionaires are stealing 50% or more of their workers labor value so that it can sit around in investment funds and stock portfolios providing nothing of value to society. And when we start to take certain other things into account it gets even worse.

There are currently over 582,000 homeless people in the United States, many of which are children (shows screenshot of data mentioned). And in the year 2020, there were more than 34 million food insecure people in the United States. That's about 10% of the population that doesn't know where their next meal is going to come from.

Now, do you know how much it would cost to end homelessness in the United States? According to the Department of Housing and Urban Development, it would cost 20 billion dollars to end homelessness in the United States.

And there are currently 770 billionaires in the United States, putting aside the fact that Elon Musk alone could end homelessness for half the cost of what he paid for Twitter. If we split it up evenly across all 770 of them, each of them would only have to pay out a lowly 26 million dollars and yet despite the ease with which they could end homelessness in the United States, billionaires are wasting their money on vanity projects like dying in a sub at the bottom of the ocean and buying Twitter.

There is no room for billionaires in an ethical society. They quite simply shouldn't exist.

His caption read "**Eat the Rich**"

I Plan to Move Abroad, Part 1

Back-to-back Testimonials by various individuals,
posted by Girl Going Around

———————

Woman 1: We can't afford our rent. We can't afford our prescriptions. We can't afford insulin. We can't afford healthcare. We can't afford our education.

Man 1: It's just so frustrating that we did everything they told us to do. We went to school, we got educated, we worked hard. We did everything they told us to do. And then when we are actually out in the world, they want to charge us 1,800 dollars for a 1-bedroom apartment, that really ain't sh*t. And then when they talk about "oh the future is gonna be great for you, you just gotta work hard" you say now "*how*?" A lot of people don't have savings, their spending it all on basic sh*t. Like, housing and groceries and what scares me the most is that more and more people are becoming aware of how more fucked it is, and all we do? We record a video, we post it on TikTok, we post it on Instagram, we post it on social media, and say "whelp I've done my part" and we close that app and we go about our day. That doesn't fix anything.

Woman 2: One of the coolest parts about being a millennial is we just got to watch our parents like try their best and be successful. Like they all had homes and 401ks and health insurance and they were like "we just did our best." And then they were telling us, they're like "just go to college and you can do anything," "if you just go to college you can do anything," so we all went to college and now we're in debt. We have no f**king money or jobs or housing. The housing market, everything sucks, and then they're like well "why didn't you go to trade school?" and we're like you told us to go to college!

Woman 3: How can you be mad at someone who literally does not have what they need to survive. When it's the corporations that have been under paying people for years. Profits are up. Productivity is up. Are wages up? No. They're not. And our money, our tax dollars, go to welfare to supplement corporations not paying people what they should.

Man 2: Some people don't wake up and the first thing on their mind is money. Everybody don't think about a dollar consistently. I gotta hustle 24/7. I gotta have 10 streams of income. I gotta learn how to flip houses. I gotta learn how to sell on Amazon. I gotta go doe-to-doe to sell vacuum cleaners. I can't just have a job and go home enjoy my money? Enjoy my time with my kids?

Woman 4: The United States, ya'll work in order to survive. Ya'll don't work in order to enjoy ya'll selves. And unfortunately, that the way the system is setup.

Woman 5: Wake up. Check your feed. Check your texts. Check your emails. Go to work. Get 100 things done. Get home late. Attempt to have energy for stuff like your kids, chores, hobbies etc. Fail miserably, feel awful and then repeat.

Podcast Skit

a TikTok scene, spoken words by *Crash Dummies Podcast*

_____

Scene: two men are hosting a podcast seated in chairs opposite of one another with microphones in front of their mouths and headphones on. The third person is a caller off-stage.

Host 1: (to caller) If you could make a new law, what would it be?

Caller: (without hesitation) You cannot be a *part-time* dopeboy. Like go big or go da f**k home.

(all three laugh)

Caller: there's no f**king way you should be a dope boy but still having to work overtime at work. F**ck it wrong with you?

Host 2: If you working with somebody and you see them selling dope on break, what you gone say to them?

Caller: Get a f**king grip. (both hosts start laughing) Grow the f**k up. (both hosts continue laughing) Get some weight. You either just gonna be Big Meech or a foot solider.

(both hosts laugh)

Host 2: I never thought about it that way.

Caller: They hit me up like bro. Don't you know such-and-such got the dope? I called, like hey bro, this such-and-such. Yeah bro, I'm out right now. (short pause) Ni**a, *why*? Apply yourself!

(both hosts laugh)

End scene.

Find Me Jose Monkey

an interactive teaching tool, by *Jose Monkey,*
Dad. Nerd. Ally.

(Man appears to be standing outside on a driving range, at night)

Man: Hey Jose Monkey, I heard you were finding people, I know you can't find us. (Man pans the background behind him. His friend photobombs with a smile)

Jose Monkey: You asked me to figure out where this video was recorded, so I did. Hi, I'm Jose Monkey and I find people that ask to be found. In yesterday's video I told you about some new tools I was learning about using for geolocation purposes, but today's video realizes on good old fashion observation and reasoning. So, what can we see?

This video appears to be have been recorded at a driving range. The video was recorded in selfie-mode, so the first thing I did was flip it horizontally so it wouldn't be mirrored. You turn the camera all around and show me the surroundings. I made note of things both inside and outside of this location. Outside, we couldn't see too much, but I noticed that off in the distance we could see a lighted sign that looks like it might be from a gas station. And to the right side, we can see a well-lit area with some kind of tall structure that I couldn't make out exactly what it was. Inside the driving range, I noticed the following details: this building has rather distinctive green walls. I also noticed these green ladder-back chairs that we can see. We have these metal-in-glass doors in the middle here, with the TV mounted above them. And we can see a US flag displayed and also another flag which I wasn't sure about but was pretty sure it was a Texas state flag.

Then I got a few more clues from the people in the video, specifically the clothing they were wearing. The person speaking in the video is wearing a Boston Red Sox hat, but the other person is wearing clothing for another team. He's wearing a Houston Astros t-shirt and hat, much like the one I'm showing here. The Astros gear and a possible Texas flag made me think this was possibly in Texas. I guess it couldv'e been Boston but, I didn't think so. Now, if you follow baseball, which I do not, then you know that there are 2 major league baseball teams in Texas, the Houston Astros and the Texas Rangers. Now I know there are many places were you have two sports teams in the same state, you get a get a bit of a divide between fans of one team versus the fans of another. And I suspected that that would be true here as well. So, if this was "Astro's country," where would it be? Well near Houston, of course. But I knew that it would extend to the surrounding areas as well. So, I tried to find some information about where you would most likely Rangers fan versus where you would find Astros fans. And I found this handy map, which suggests that I should be looking in Southeast Texas. So, I brought up Google Maps, zoomed in on Texas, and started looking for driving ranges in the place where you would find the largest concentration of Astros fans. And I got some results right away. You were at the sixth one that I checked.

You're at Mulligan's Golf Center, in Angleton, Tx.

The Google street view of this location shows the building still under construction. But I didn't really know what the front of the building looked like anyway so it probably didn't matter. I was to see some user submitted photos on the Google Maps entry for this location though. This one showed me a view down the driving range, in which I could see a lighted sign that looked to me like it might be the same one from your video. But this photo was really the jackpot. I could see that *all* of the details matched what was in your video. We had the green walls, the green ladder-back chairs, we had the metal-in-glass doors with the TV mounted over them. The flags. Everything was just like in your video. By the way, that lighted sign that we saw was for a Love's truck stop slash Carl's Jr. And I'm pretty sure that that well-lit area was a nearby Golf Coast car dealer. I think the tall structure we seeing in the video was probably their flag pole.

Guys please like and share. and if anybody else would like for me to figure out where their video was recorded, send me a video and where you say "find me Jose Monkey," or something like that on camera, or hold up a sign that says something similar. And don't forget to tag me in the comment on that video.

PAUSE (THE VIDEO) TO READ THIS:

- You must be 18 or older to play. If you're under 18, do not ask!
- If you want me to locate a video, record a video where you say "Find me josemonkey" on-camera or hold up a sign that says something like that. Also, tag me in a comment on that video.
- Do no tag me in someone else's videos.
- By tagging me in a video, you are asking me to publicly disclose the location in the video and giving me a non-exclusive, royalty-free license to use the video.
- Pleas tag me in videos that are recorded in public spaces. I don't want to reveal your home address or any other location you would prefer to remain private.

Focus on Money

spoken words by *Emily Bonani*

———————

Stop focusing on dating,

focus on money!

You are poor,

you are poor.

You are broke and poor.

The only Chase you should be texting is the bank.

Focus on how you're going to make money

and how you're gonna be happy doing that.

You wanna find the love of your life?

Money will make that easier!

Travelers Beware

spoken words by Keith aka *Foolishness*

<u>List of Hotels</u>
1. Hilton
2. Wyndham
3. Days Inn
4. Super 8
5. Best Western
6. Red Lion
7. Marriot
8. Choice Hotels
9. Extended Stay America
10. Motel 6

Yo, TikTok. I know a lot of ya'll travel, a lot of ya'll like to be on the road and a lot of ya'll get hotels and Airbnbs, but what i need ya'll to know is this is a list of hotels (reads out the list). What do all these hotels have in common? They're all being sued right now for human trafficking. They have been *participants* in human trafficking but wait, that's not all.

In some of these hotels, they have found tunnels. In the closets. That go underground, that lead to missing children. Aye, do your own research. As you can see right here inserts screenshot behind him) the lawsuits against major hotel company including these (Wyndham Hotels and Resorts, Red Roof Inns, and Choice Hotels International are mentioned in the article) for allowing trafficking to occur on their property and profiting from human trafficking.

Also, these hidden cameras (shows a small device with a pinhole camera lens) have been found in a lot of these hotels as well. The traffickers use these cameras to spy on you and to see who they can kidnap. This is a coat hanger. This is a camera that looks like a plane screw (shows device). You would never know that you have that, you have, that… people. You have to check your room for cameras.

Also, be aware of hotels that offer free shampoo and some conditioners. Because a lot of these containers will have shampoo in them but the base of the container is a whole camera system (shows a image of the device mentioned). so be careful at Airbnbs and at hotels everywhere. You can actually buy a device that will scan a room and let you know if there are cameras in the room. And it will show you where the cameras are. And for reference, this is a hotel in Florida that had a hole in the closet that they went through and they found children waayyyyy down that tunnel, where they kidnapped people who checked into these hotels (shows a still image of a hole in the ground).

Your Body is a Vehicle

spoken words by *Zach Pogrob,*
of Behavior Hack

———————

When you feel off, turn your body on.
Lift, run, train.

When you overthink, turn your body off.
Sit. Journal. Meditate.

Your body isn't just a home, it's a vehicle.
Use it to change yourself, physically and mentally.

A Relationship

spoken word by *Trace Ellis Ross*

———————

I would love a relationship, that makes me life better than it is.

I have no interest being in a relationship, just to be in a relationship.

The truth is, that like, I'm a rare breed, so like, there may not be a match that's a rare breed for a while.

Message to a Black Girl

spoken words by *jaebabylacy*

You don't have to be friendly.

I just want to say that, there are so many people that tell me after we become friends, "I thought you didn't like me," "I thought like." (sigh) Why? "Oh because, you were giving me a mean mug." "Mmm, was I? Or was I just walking to class? Was I, or was I just doing my work" like (side eye) people often internalize black, especially dark-skinned women, they often internalize our facial expressions and they feel like things we do is against them and take everything to heart, in reality we are just minding our business.

And I'm just letting you know it's okay to not look nice. It's ok to not smile (fakes smile) all the time, and be fake. You don't have to do that. You don't have to overcompensate. You don't have to be overly nice. You don't have to be like overly open. That's not your job to make people feel comfortable with you.

Sign,
-A Black Girl

Getting "Flew Out"

spoken words by *Jordyn*,
of *Jordanthoughts*

Woman in audience: …but if you want to spend your dime just know that I'm not on that.

Jordyn: That don't matter because even if you say something, let me tell you, I sold cars. I was top salesman in the car industry and one of the tactics that we would do customer would call in. (Picks up pretend phone) "Hey, ya'll got this truck here?" If I tell a customer no, the customer is not coming into the dealership. You can't sell them unless they're there at the dealership, so even if you ain't got the truck… (pretends to pick up phone again) "yeah, we got it. What time you coming?"

Boom, they get there, customer be mad cause the truck ain't there, but then you sell them on something else and they leave with a car. So, you can tell him that I'm not doing nothing, a skilled dude will say okay. I'm good with that. Get you there, and then flip the switch on you and start pressuring you to do something. Pay your own way is real simple.

Woman: cause I ain't gone lie ya'll I used to be real, *real* broke and I ain't had no money so I know I was going out there really on his dime to pay for everything. I'm talkin' bout I ain't even had no money to check my luggage.

Jordyn: (shakes her head) Yeah. That's a dangerous game to play.

Woman: I made sure I had a round-trip to get home.

Jordyn: Yeah but even then, what if he decided to take you somewhere right and drop you off and tell you to find your way back? You ain't got no money and you got to wait on a day to leave. What if you miss your flight? As a matter of fact, for him doing something to intentionally make you miss your flight? Now, what you gone do? You see the thing is never put yourself in a position where you ain't got no out. If you gone let a dude fly you out, always make sure you got money. You don't want no male to have power over you at all. **Period**.

Surrender

spoken words by *Styx River,*
artist

You're trying to harddddd.
You gotta remember the path of least resistance being effortless.

I thought we said we not chasing no more,
but here you are, trotting.

Come on now, don't chase. Attract, be a magnet, okay?
No more chasing, no more forcing.

Flow, and let it go.
If it comes to you, it's yours. If it don't, let it go.

Real Things I heard as a Paramedic

spoken words by *FireDeptChronicles,*
firefighter/comedian

Scene: woman is giving birth and being assisted by the paramedics, all the viewer can see are her feet. One paramedic is knelt, the other is standing, coaching the women through the birth.

Paramedic 1: I can see the head. A couple more big pushes and the baby is going to come out, alright?

Paramedic 2: (to man entering the doorway) Oh hey, you must be the boyfriend?

Boyfriend: yeah, yeah, yeah, uuh, I sw the trucks outside..

Paramedic 1: (to the woman) good…

Boyfriend: is she okay? (pointing to his girlfriend off-camera)

Paramedic 2: Dude, she's doing great, man. The baby is almost here.

Boyfriend: What the…

Paramedic 1: (to the woman) Good.

Boyfriend gasps.

Paramedic 2 celebrates.

Paramedic 1: It's a boy! (baby starts crying in the background)

Boyfriend: (starts counting using his fingers looking confused)

Paramedic 2: Hey listen bro. I know this feels completely overwhelming right now, but don't worry man. You're gonna be an awesome dad.

Boyfriend: No, it's not that. I just got back from college, and uhhh… and I've been gone for a year.

All at once, Paramedic 2's face drops, Boyfriend is frozen, Paramedic 1 is too stunned to speak, Baby stops crying.

Paramedic 2: Okay (claps hand together) Who's ready to go to the hospital?

A Brief History in Florida Tourism

spoken words by *Tabitha*,
Political Analyst

———————

Remember when the NAACP put out its travel advisory, warning black people not to travel to the state of Florida because of the hostility of the government in Florida?

If you missed the notice, here's the notice, you can go on over to the NAACP website to read it (puts up screenshot of the logo from the site). After the NAACP issued that travel advisory, Ron Desantis was doing some type of press conference and he was asked about it.

Here's what he said:

"What a joke. What a joke. Yeah, we'll see how, we'll see how effective that is. It's a pure stunt. And fine, if you want to waste your time on a stunt, that's fine. Look, I, I, I got, I'm not wasting my time on your stunts, okay. I'm gonna make sure that we're getting, get things done here. And we're gonna continue to make this state a great state."

Well, black folks at that point were like, "well baby, we can show you better than we can tell you." And then not too long after that, I mean immediately after that, other organizations that represent other marginalized communities started to issue travel advisories for the state of Florida. Equality Florida issued a travel advisory. And the Human Rights Campaign joined in with Equality Florida and issued a travel advisory for the state of Florida. And there were other organizations that represent black people, that represent the LGBTQIA community, that also represent the Hispanic community, they all started issuing travel advisories for the state of Florida.

And then all of you all started canceling your vacations to Florida. And simultaneously, while all of that was happening, Ron Desantis went over to his Twitter account and tweeted this (shows image of the Tweet with data for travel in Florida). As if these numbers were going to last forever. No, baby because now this is what's happening…

Conventions are pulling out in Central Florida. They're also pulling out down in Broward County, which is South Florida. Remember when Disney said "I'm am sick of your 'ish," and they pulled their 1-billion dollar project out of the state of Florida? Not to mention, all of the immigrants that were working in the state of Florida, you know, your fruit pickers, your construction workers, your hotel workers, your kitchen workers, your babysitters, yeah, they all left the state of Florida.

(Picture of Ron Desantis smiling in a article in the background) And now, the state of Florida is starting to feel it. The experts are panicking because the tourism in Florida is dropping.

(Tabitha laughs, diabolically)

The Company

spoken words by *Albaner C. Eugene Jr.*

The scripture that comes to mind is "bad company corrupts good morals, corrupts good character." I hate to say this but I found it to be true.

You really become what you hang around. It's very painful to come to realization that there are some people you just can't continue to associate with because their gonna become a hindrance to you. Because they will become a detriment or a danger to you. Even though simple communication can be presented, if it's not like an abusive thing. And that's why I say it's very important in this life as we're doing life, not talking about the people you run into here and there. I'm talking about people you do life with, that you choose these people wisely because they say if you show me the 5 people you spend the most time with, I can show you your future.

People that have lost their lives innocently by association, (touches heart) that's hurtful, by being at the wrong place at the wrong time with the wrong crowd, that's painful. You have to have an honest conversation that it might be time that you may need to just take a step back, go (y)our separate ways or just really communicate that you know, the place you're in your life right now, you can't get involved in a lot of that activity no more. And you can even share with them this is what God is doing in your life, they may not understand it, but you still have to move.

And before you get resentful of the. bad company, do your due diligence communicate and separate.

Who You Are

spoken words by *Caroline A, Wanga,*
of WangaWoman

———————

Who you are is *who* you are.

If you cannot be who you are,

where you are,

you must change *where* you are,

not *who* you are.

Untitled
spoken words by *21 Savage,*
Rapper

I'd rather have loyalty than love,
cause love don't mean jack.
See, love is just a feeling
You can love somebody
and still stab 'em in they back.

It don't really take much to love,
You can love somebody,
just by being attached
See, *loyalty* is an action
You can love me or hate me,
and still have my back.

Made in the USA
Coppell, TX
17 July 2023